For André and Noelle

Library of Congress catalog card number: 2021932191
ISBN: 978-1-7353521-6-9 (Paperback)
978-1-7353521-7-6 (Hardback)

Formatting by Praise Saflor

André Goes Fishing

Written by

Mikaela Wilson

Illustrated by

Pardeep Mehra

Art Direction and Storyboards by

Mikaela Wilson

"Time to go fishing!" shouts André's dad.

André is excited!
He has never been fishing before.

André puts on his new fishing vest and his new fishing hat.

He grabs his new fishing pole and his new fishing tackle box. He is ready to go.

"Let's pack it up," says André's dad.

Suddenly...they stop!

André points to the sky.
"Look at those dark clouds!"

Suddenly it starts to rain. Big raindrops are landing on his new fishing vest and his new fishing hat.

"Oh no! What are we going to do?" asks André.

"I want to go fishing!"

André's dad thinks for a minute.
"I have an idea," he says.
"Let's go back inside."

André and his dad dry themselves off. "We're going to use our imaginations," Dad says.

Dad climbs onto the bed.
"This will be our fishing boat!"

André climbs up next to his dad. Dad throws some pillows on the floor. "Okay, André, these are our big fish."

"We need a fishing pole!" exclaims André. "You're right," Dad says. "This will be our fishing pole. Let's see what we can catch!"

André casts his fishing line for the very first time…

...out into the water.

"I think you caught something!" Dad calls out.

André pulls on the fishing
pole as hard as he can.

"WOW!" shouts André's dad.
"Look at the huge fish you caught!"

"Let's catch more fish!"
André exclaims.

This time André feels something very strong.
"Dad, I got something big!"

"Pull it up!" Dad shouts.

As they pull the fishing line up, André can't believe his eyes...

"It's...a...**SHARK!**" André shouts.

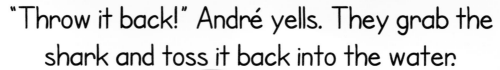

"Throw it back!" André yells. They grab the shark and toss it back into the water.

André and his dad catch many more fish.

They even catch an octopus
and a big sea monster.

After a long day of fishing, André is tired.
"Thanks for taking me fishing today,"
he says, smiling.

André never knew rainy days
could be so much fun.

André

Noelle

Dear Reader,

I hope you enjoyed reading this book!
If you have a moment to spare, please drop a quick
review on Amazon. I'm grateful for all the feedback!
If you have any questions or comments please email
mikaelawilsonbooks@gmail.com

Be the first to know about new book releases
and grab your free coloring pages at
www.mikaelawilsonbooks.com

 @mikaelawilsonbooks

 Mikaela Wilson Books

 @MikaelaWilsonBooks

About the Author
Mikaela Wilson

Mikaela Wilson is an author on a mission to bring fun, entertaining and meaningful stories to children's lives. In addition to working full-time as an IT Application Analyst, she is a wife and a mother of two young children. After reading countless children's books with her kids, she saw a need for more diversity in children's books and decided to create her own. The *André and Noelle* books are inspired by her two children and modeled after her own multicultural family. Mikaela hopes her books will be timeless and families can read and enjoy them for years to come.

About the Illustrator
Pardeep Mehra

Pardeep Mehra is the founder of Pencil Master Digital Studio, a family-owned business employing a large group of talented artists providing end-to-end illustration and publishing services. For more than 15 years, Pardeep has been providing his keen eye, visualization and digital art skills to create books that delight children all over the world. Pardeep lives in India with his wife and daughter. For more info visit www.pencilmasterdigi.com

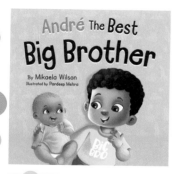
André The Best **Big Brother**
By Mikaela Wilson
Illustrated by Pardeep Mehra

Noelle The Best **Big Sister**
By Mikaela Wilson
Illustrated by Pardeep Mehra

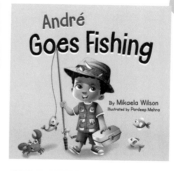
André **Goes Fishing**
By Mikaela Wilson
Illustrated by Pardeep Mehra

Noelle **Bakes a Cake**
By Mikaela Wilson
Illustrated by Pardeep Mehra

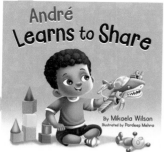
André **Learns to Share**
By Mikaela Wilson
Illustrated by Pardeep Mehra

Noelle **Goes to the Museum**
By Mikaela Wilson
Illustrated by Pardeep Mehra

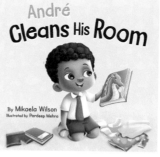
André **Cleans His Room**
By Mikaela Wilson
Illustrated by Pardeep Mehra

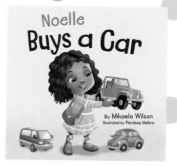
Noelle **Buys a Car**
By Mikaela Wilson
Illustrated by Pardeep Mehra

André and the **Special Gift**
By Mikaela Wilson
Illustrated by Pardeep Mehra

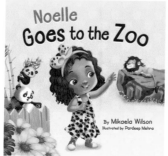
Noelle **Goes to the Zoo**
By Mikaela Wilson
Illustrated by Pardeep Mehra

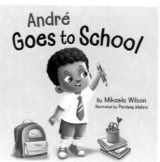
André **Goes to School**
By Mikaela Wilson
Illustrated by Pardeep Mehra

Noelle **Goes on a Picnic**
By Mikaela Wilson
Illustrated by Pardeep Mehra

Noelle and the **Haunted House**
By Mikaela Wilson
Illustrated by Pardeep Mehra

Scan the QR Code
to find these
titles and more!

MIKAELA WILSON BOOKS

Made in United States
Troutdale, OR
10/18/2023

13802991R00021